SCOTTISH TALES

Edited By Donna Samworth

First published in Great Britain in 2018 by:

 Young**Writers**

Young Writers
Remus House
Coltsfoot Drive
Peterborough
PE2 9BF
Telephone: 01733 890066
Website: www.youngwriters.co.uk

FOREWORD

Young Writers was created in 1991 with the express purpose of promoting and encouraging creative writing. Each competition we create is tailored to the relevant age group, hopefully giving each pupil the inspiration and incentive to create their own piece of work, whether it's a poem or a short story. We truly believe that seeing their work in print gives pupils a sense of achievement and pride in their work and themselves.

For Stranger Sagas, we challenged secondary school pupils to write a mini saga – a story in just 100 words. They were given the choice of eight story starters to give their imaginations a kick start:

- At birth everyone's tattooed with their date of death. Mine's dated yesterday...

- The last thing I remember is...

- I unravel the family portrait; if these are my parents, who's that downstairs...?

- I need to tell someone the truth before it's too late...

- The sun was blazing; I took out the map, I must be close...

- There was a noise coming from the basement...

- We watched from the space station as Earth exploded...

- I got off the plane, the terminal was empty...

They could use any one of these to begin their story, or alternatively they could choose to go it alone and create that all important first line themselves. With bizarre beginnings, mysterious middles and enigmatic endings, the resulting tales in this collection cover a range of genres and showcase the talent of the next generation. From fun to frightening to the weird and wonderful, these mini sagas are sure to keep you entertained and take you to strange new worlds.

CONTENTS

Regan Galletly (12)	59
Ben Keenan (11)	60
William Lawless (12)	61
Cameron Dougall (12)	62
Olivia Stewart (11)	63
Connor Davey (12)	64
Madison MacDonald (12)	65
Roan Buckham (12)	66
Charlotte Makin (12)	67
Lauren Kirkham (12)	68
Gregor Hunter (12)	69
Ashly Kidd (11)	70
Lottie Tyler Mears (12)	71
Carla Shaw (12)	72
Amber Wilson (11)	73
Nicole Davidson (12)	74
Angus Tulloch (12)	75

Inverness High School, Inverness

Kieran Loughhead (13)	76
Paige Morrison (14)	77

Lenzie Academy, Lenzie

Dylan McCabe (15)	78
Aiden Glasswell (14)	79
Aaron Wilkie (14)	80
Jack Cullen (15)	81
Sean Bill McLaughlin (15)	82
Robbie Andrew Goodfellow (15)	83

Queen Margaret Academy, Ayr

Heather Amy Needham (15)	84
Kaloyan Galev (15)	85
Benjamin Cochrane (15)	86

St George's School For Girls, Edinburgh

Hattie Eleanor Fowler (11)	87
Isla Macfadyen (11)	88
Heidi Masters (11)	89
Iona Talbot Rice (11)	90

Clara Anna Elisabeth Ahnert (11)	91
Charlotte Earl (11)	92
Zainab Shahid Hafeez (11)	93
Rona Marshall (11)	94
Maira Lakshmy Ratnarajah (11)	95
Kate Green (11)	96
Eliza Gardiner (11)	97
Isabella Grahamslaw (11)	98
Honor Simpson (11)	99
Chloe Taylor (11)	100
Orla McKenzie Gray (11)	101
Rosie Simpson (11)	102
Anaysa Kaddeer (11)	103
Lois Norrie (11)	104
Sara Qayyum (11)	105
Arabella Simpson (11)	106

Stewarton Academy, Stewarton

Aadam Saafi (14)	107
Anna Sinclair (13)	108
Andrew Lancaster (14)	109
Matthew Lyon (14)	110
Max Burns (14)	111
Orla MacDonald (14)	112
Benjamin Michael Dalley (14)	113
Rowan McClure (14)	114
Ella Duncan (14)	115
Grant McClure (14)	116
Sam Speirs (14)	117
Bryn Harzmeyer (14)	118
Morgan Daniel Cumming (14)	119

The Gordon Schools, Huntly

Bente van West (12)	120
Lauren Ferguson (13)	121
Freya Helen Tamiozzo Wilson (13)	122
Lucy Barclay (13)	123
Callum Paterson (12)	124
Laura Brown (13)	125
Elise Desgouttes (12)	126

Thomas Hinton (12)	127
Samara Irvine (11)	128
Scott Milne (12)	129
Rosa Bressers (13)	130
Innes Cranna (13)	131
Sam Mitchell (12)	132
Ailie Maclennan (12)	133
Alice Wilson (12)	134
Jade Mackie (13)	135
Rebecca Watson (11)	136
Candice Lauw (12)	137
Ross MacPherson (12)	138
Rona Duncan (13)	139
Thomas Eadon (12)	140
Lewis Murray (12)	141
Emma Buyers (12)	142

THE MINI SAGAS

The Date Of My Death

At birth everyone's tattooed with their date of death. Mine's dated yesterday, at precisely 12.30pm. My older sister Ellie and I were playing on the swings in the park. We were going as high as we could whilst standing up. Suddenly, I lost my grip. Then blackness. There was the sound of a scream. Ellie was standing over me, tears streaming down her face. I wrapped my arm around my sister's neck but she didn't notice. Gingerly, I stood up. My body was on the ground, lifeless. "I'm here!" I screamed. Ellie didn't notice and continued cradling my dead body.

Isla McNair (12)
Alford Academy, Alford

A Familiar Mystery

Sweat trickled down my forehead like treacle, each drop weighed me down, further and further into the ground. My legs trembled with fear as I mustered the strength to lift myself upright. The tall, withered oak trees surrounding me felt like they were closing in. Every cautious step I took was like climbing the tracks to the top of a steep roller coaster. The feeling of familiarity grew like bacteria, doubling, tripling in size. Suddenly, my stomach dropped, everything around me began to be violently sucked into a deep, dark, black hole, vacuuming me into an abyss of nothingness...

Alejandra Paola Delgado (16)
Alford Academy, Alford

Death Day

At birth, everyone's tattooed with their date of death. Mine's dated yesterday, 15/04/17... My fourteenth birthday. The date was clearly marked on the inside of my wrist, it was the day I died. I stood on the train, my wrist covered and tightly held to hide the faded tattoo. A young girl and two men dressed in suits sat opposite. The girl sat between the men, her head held down. I couldn't see her face. She slumped to the floor, exposing her face. Her hand fell, displaying the date on her wrist... 14/04/17... I glanced over and saw my face...

Faith Woolsey (14)
Alford Academy, Alford

The Figure In The Window

I ran down the uneven path that led away from the spooky mansion. The crumbling manor towered high, the large oak doors looked majestic. My face was etched with horror as a grey figure stared out of the window, watching with amusement. I felt a sudden rage towards the creature but it soon evaporated as it glared at me, fiercely. Creaking trees around the side of the building were being buffeted around wildly and the leaves were creating a funnel. Suddenly, the creature was gone. I felt petrified. A loud, echoing growl made me freeze... I knew I was dead.

Keira Trudgill (12)
Alford Academy, Alford

The Beast From The Basement

I grabbed my torch and tiptoed to the basement door. The noise was louder now, echoing in my ears. I slowly opened the door. Suddenly, red hit me. The smell of burning engulfed me, my eyes were streaming. The eyes of this beast were smokey-black, only visible because of their glow. I stepped back in horror. The noise was so high-pitched. Now it was unbearable. I fell back in fear, hitting my head on the doorstep behind me. The beast came closer, I could tell in my dizziness. It growled at me, spitting in anger, "Leave me alone!"

Verity Harvey (13)
Alford Academy, Alford

Asylum

The last thing I remember is peripheral vision blurring and my head hitting the floor with an almighty thud. I woke up in a white room, with two perfectly parallel windows. My hands were tied behind my back in a straightjacket and my hair was neatly plaited behind me. There was a mirror on the wall, a plain acrylic mirror and even the thought of it made me shudder with obstinate dread. I got up and walked backwards towards the mirror, it was rather hard as I'd had a concussion yesterday. Nevertheless, I turned to face my own reflection...

Hope McCartney (12)
Alford Academy, Alford

Expired

It began when they took over, nobody stood a chance. They brought weapons we could only dream of creating. They made the system and we're forced to follow it. If you resist, well, you're already dead. They'll do things worse than kill. They erase your entire being, loved ones stop knowing who you were. It will be like you never existed. At birth, everyone's tattooed with their date of death on their biceps. I was meant to die yesterday, and now the government will hunt me down. Why? I am the girl who's out of date. I am expired...

Chloé Crossland (14)
Alford Academy, Alford

Earth's Story

We watched from the space station as Earth exploded... The devastation spread across our faces as we realised how much we'd lost; our homes, our countries and our families. Out of instinct, I went to hug my mum, then I realised she wasn't there. The only person beside me was my sister, we had stuck together since we were born. We had no one else, so we had no choice. All the way through life, we had shared everything, like secrets and friends. We were inseparable. I turned to my sister, it was like nothing had changed, but it had...

Kathryn Nicol (12)
Alford Academy, Alford

Untitled

At birth, everyone's tattooed with their date of death. Mine's dated yesterday. I woke up in a bed, surrounded by a plastic dome. In walked three men wearing white. "Where am I?" I screamed, hoping for a reply.
"This is your end and your beginning," they replied. They marched out as they were to go to battle. I turned and saw millions of beds like mine either side, full of men, women and children. Some I knew for ages, until they'd died, but I'm not not actually dead and neither are they. What is this...?

Ben Geddes (13)
Alford Academy, Alford

The Man Who Went Out Of Date

At birth, everyone's tattooed with their date of death. Mine was yesterday. An alien race, called the Combine, took over Earth with plans to enslave the human race. They put things into the water and food to make us forget who we were. They packed us into huge cities with big walls to stop people from leaving and other things from coming in. The cities reeked of poverty. No one made money any more and the only people with proper homes were working with the Combine. However, I was more concerned about myself and the people knocking on my door...

Cameron Clark (14)
Alford Academy, Alford

Barren Desert

The sun was blazing. I took out the map, I must be close...
The desert was scorching hot. However, still I was
determined to get to the village on the map. If I stopped
now, I would surely lose consciousness but I was just too
dehydrated. I took a sip from my flask and when I did, I saw
the village one or two miles away. Suddenly, as I started to
walk to the village, I saw stars out of the corners of my eyes.
Meaning only one thing... I was starting to lose
consciousness. It was too late...

Calum Scott (14)
Alford Academy, Alford

Night Of The Earth

We watched from the space station as the Earth exploded. It brought a tear to my eye, seeing the planet I grew up on explode. All those memories on my home planet flooded back to me. I can't remember how I got here, I just know I'm lucky to be alive and safe. Suddenly, thoughts flooded through my mind. Why am I here? The last thing I remember is being in my kitchen and then *bang*, I'm here! I felt someone breathing on the back of my neck. Slowly and silently, I began to turn around...

Eva Lewis (12)
Alford Academy, Alford

The Little Rusty Robot

I hadn't been on the space station for long since the evacuation. I decided to look around. I saw a peculiar object from the corner of my eye, as it flew past the space station. I tried to ignore it at first but the tapping at the window was impossible to ignore. I felt I was the only person on the station that could hear it. The noise that this little, rusty robot was making with its hand against the window, started to get louder but slower. I turned around and people were starting to disappear with every tap...

Darcy Ann Eaton (14)
Alford Academy, Alford

The Burgundy-Eyed Thing In The Basement

There was a noise coming from the basement. I grabbed a knife from the kitchen. As I walked down into the basement, I saw two glowing burgundy eyes. As I turned on the light, they were gone. I told mum about my encounter in the basement. She told me to never go down there again. After yesterday, things got worse. I started seeing a woman in a white, ripped hospital gown and screaming at three in the morning. On Friday, I was petrified. Mum said not to go to school but I went...

Sophie Middleton (12)
Alford Academy, Alford

Untitled

At birth, everyone's tattooed with their date of death. Mine's dated yesterday. I woke up as normal and walked downstairs. "Morning," I said. I got no reply. I repeated myself and tapped my mum on the shoulder. I got no reaction. I walked back upstairs and sat on my bed, puzzled. Mum was coming upstairs. I heard her crying. She came into my room, stood in the centre, looked around and cried louder. Tears were a constant flow down her face. I looked in the mirror... There was no reflection.

Lyndsey Brown (14)
Alford Academy, Alford

Terminal

I got off the plane, the terminal was empty. I looked behind me, I swear there were others on the plane. I continuously moved forward, looking around me. It looked like the place had been deserted for years. I moved swiftly around the airport. I started to panic a bit. Suddenly, I heard it... I quickly turned and... Nothing. I walked on, being more careful and as soon as I turned a corner, it was lying in the middle of the floor... Had I been taken somewhere I'm not meant to be?

Sandy Watt (14)
Alford Academy, Alford

The Expiration Date

It started when I got a goodbye letter. I was on the run from the government. I went to see if my good friend Jasper could help me get away from all this chaos. It's been a week since my expiration date and Jasper has hidden me well. He was good company and he treated me well. "I don't know him. I will look for the runaway," that's all I heard. Little did I know, he was part of the government and my one-week expiration date had just expired...

Leah Fennelly (13)
Alford Academy, Alford

Sctrailla

I fell asleep in my warm, comfy bed, then I woke up somewhere strange. It felt weird, it had strange-looking people. All of a sudden, someone walked by, staring straight into my eyes. These people didn't have noses or lips and they were grey, with warts all over. The next thing I knew, I was in a strange-looking house with metal bars everywhere... I worried about what would happen next. A strange person walked in and started describing me: "Brown hair, blue eyes, no freckles, average height. Earth!"
"Now I know where I am!" I screamed, "In Sctrailla! Yes!"

Jaimee Adams (11)
Ayr Academy, Ayr

The Mysterious Figure

The last thing I remember is... There was a knock at the door and now I am at this strange place. I hear footsteps creeping outside the chamber I'm confined in, but who is making them? The only other noise I can hear is the droning of the dazzling light above me. *Buzz. Buzz.* I hear somebody clattering keys, then a key going into the lock. The door handle turns and the door slowly creeps open. Panic quickens my heartbeat and my mind fills with dread. Out of nowhere, the light flickers off and then there's a mysterious, dark figure...

Oliver Stewart (13)
Ayr Academy, Ayr

Fear

I unravelled the family portrait; if these were my parents, then who was downstairs? I slowly waddled out of my bedroom and crept downstairs to see who it was. Taking a peak, I saw my mum and a wave of relief went over me. I went down to greet her. "Hey Mum!" I said as I strolled into the kitchen.

"Hey sweetie," she replied.

Before I continued talking, my phone rang. I answered it...

"Honey? I'm nearly home, can you unlock the door for me?" A chill went down my spine. The person in the kitchen wasn't my mum...

Joey Demarco (12)
Ayr Academy, Ayr

A New Day

At birth, everybody is tattooed with their date of death. Mine's dated yesterday... I suddenly woke up this morning asking myself, "How am I still alive?" It was the same old broken bed, in the same old dusty bedroom. Just a new day. Was the date mixed up? Am I going to die today? These questions went through my head all morning. I got up, got changed into my usual clothes and went outside. Everybody was miserable, as usual, but they looked slightly sadder. Nobody said hello or good morning. Then it occurred to me... I actually wasn't alive.

Abigail Kennedy Ramsey (12)
Ayr Academy, Ayr

Robot Girl

I went down the stairs and had breakfast then went for a quick shower. When I was washing my arms, I noticed something; my death date was passed. I dried myself as quickly as I could and went downstairs. "Mum, *Mum!*" I said, hurriedly. "My death date was yesterday! Why am I still alive?" My mum sat me down.

She said solemnly, "I am sorry to say, you're a robot. When me and your dad were younger, we couldn't have babies, so the hospital gave us you. You will live forever because you are a human robot..."

Megan Woods (12)

Ayr Academy, Ayr

22

In The Wall

I unravelled the family portrait; if they were my parents, then who was that downstairs? They look nothing like my mum and dad. I went down the stairs and my other mother was making dinner. She started to peel. I couldn't speak. I went into the living room and I heard someone shouting my name. I shouted, "Hello!" but nobody answered. I started to look for the voice, it was in the wall so I started to rip it open. I saw them for the first time. I tried to rip some more but I couldn't reach them...

Miah Harvey (12)
Ayr Academy, Ayr

The End?

We watched from the space station as Earth exploded... or so we thought. When Earth's debris disappeared, we saw another world that looked like Earth, so we decided to go check it out. When I got outside, I noticed there were no humans or man-made structures, only large jungles, sandy beaches, grassy plains and mountains. No animals in sight. Then I heard it... a loud roar. I saw a T-rex! This planet was still in the dinosaur age. I ran but it was faster than me. Then everything went black. There were no more noises, only a black void...

Jack Scott (14)
Ayr Academy, Ayr

Suspension

... It's a weird noise, almost like a baby's faint cry. I slowly crept downstairs, my heart pumping out of my chest. As I was tiptoeing, not daring to make a sound, it got louder. I screeched at the top of my lungs, with fear shaking my voice, "Who are you?" Suddenly, it stopped. No screaming, crying or moaning. Silence... I dared not to breathe as I crawled out of the house. Suddenly, I heard a tremendous explosion from my basement. The explosion blasted my front door open with wildfire. An unknown figure stood before me...

Holli Donaghy (12)
Ayr Academy, Ayr

The Killer

I got off the plane and the terminal was empty, except for a man in all black. he was laughing, with blood all over him and then something behind him moved. It was a person, they were barely alive! Then the man turned around. He killed him brutally then turned back to me and walked towards me. I started backing away but he chased.
Then something buzzed past me and got the man on the leg. Then people ran past me! The man's friends came with knives and they were bloody. They all charged speedily and then I blacked out...

Steven Scott (14)
Ayr Academy, Ayr

Lies

I stared at the woman in the portrait; her long, blonde hair was falling like a waterfall over her shoulders, covering part of her naturally highlighted face. My eyes drifted to the tall man in the photo; his sharp jawline so clean cut, it could slice a plank of wood in half. Then I noticed the eyes, both of them had eyes that were the same startling, olive-green as mine. I suddenly noticed a young girl that the dad was holding. She had long skinny arms and long, blonde hair, exactly like me and the beautiful woman in the photo...

Freya McCormick (12)
Ayr Academy, Ayr

Green!

... A strange crashing sound that sent shivers down my spine. I slowly walked towards the door, where a green glow came from below. I slowly opened the creaking door. I shivered, too afraid to scream, not wanting to make a noise. I walked slowly down the old, wooden stairs to the bottom. The smell was horrible, like chemicals. I heard groans and saw green. This green would give you a headache. It was so bad that you couldn't see anything but green. Someone screamed a high-pitched scream for help, it sounded like a little girl.

Caitlin McKnight (14)
Ayr Academy, Ayr

The Family Portrait

I sat on my bed, confused about the portrait. I snuck downstairs and the people I thought were my parents were eating my animals! "Mum, Dad, what are you doing?" I screamed. They didn't answer. I saw them stop and fall asleep. I ran upstairs to my bedroom and locked the door. When I looked myself up, it said I had been missing for... 250 years! This had to be a dream! In the portrait, I was faded and my feet were gone. Were my real family dead or was *I* dead? Wait... what is that? "Aaaah!"

Leah Broadley (12)
Ayr Academy, Ayr

Nightmare

The last thing I remember is... a loud gunshot that sounded like it was right outside my house and now I'm in what looks to be a very dark and creepy dungeon. There was this revolting smell in the air. It smelt like rotten flesh. I kept hearing lights flickering and metal hitting against metal, like someone was trying to make a weapon. I started to panic as the banging got louder. I was trying to find a way out. All of a sudden, a door swung open and I woke up. Was it just a dream, or reality?

Ryan Wheble (13)
Ayr Academy, Ayr

The Truth

I need to tell someone the truth before its's too late. About the horrors about to happen. The Earth is going to become a second sun. When everyone finds out my truth, they all run away. I absolutely hate the way I was born. The Earth is already burning red, deep inside. I keep trying to tell everyone about the end of the Earth and then I find someone who doesn't run away. "Hello, son. Do you no longer recognise your dad?" and then I noticed; he was the Devil. He was destroying the Earth, with me included...

Devan Davis Andrew (12)
Ayr Academy, Ayr

Silence

No one was about but all the lights were on. I saw a dark, lurking figure coming towards me. I shouted, "Is someone there?" but I got no answer. Then I heard banging; it was getting louder, like an unfamiliar drum. Then 100 people or more came running towards me... but it was not people, it was zombies! They had blood all over them. It smelt like a bin lorry and the sight was even worse. I had no time to lose. I saw a room. I went in to it and prayed that they would not come in...

Dean Tyson (14)
Ayr Academy, Ayr

The Terminal

I decided to walk on. It looked normal but hollow. I smelt a really weird stench that reminded me of death. It got stronger and I started to panic. I suddenly saw a lot of men standing there talking, then they dropped to the floor. I shouted, "Hello, anyone there?" I got no reply. Only silence. Moments later, a large group of SWAT burst through the windows and doors. They ran past and told me to get on the ground. I followed their instructions and dropped on the ground, trembling with fear and horror...

Marc Alexander Reid (13)
Ayr Academy, Ayr

Day 13

It was all my fault. I just wanted to know the answer and now I'm in more trouble than ever before. Everyone I know is dead and I'm on the ISS with my dog. I thought I was the only person left in the human race but then I remembered the prisoners and the whole ship began to shake... *It* was back and after me again. I screamed as my only defence and jumped quickly into the escape pod but it wouldn't close. *It* was blocking the door! I scrambled to get away but I was unsuccessful...

Carly Hood (11)
Ayr Academy, Ayr

Gone

The last thing I remember is being taken away from my home and taken to a hospital that was hiding a lab for experiments. One day, they did one of these experiments on me. They implanted a chip in my brain and it gave me powers. I could speak telepathically and move objects with my mind. I could also get inside minds and make them see whatever I wanted. Once, two people dressed in white came and took me from the room. I lashed out, I used my powers. I blinked. When I looked around, everyone was gone.

Thomas Lindores (12)
Ayr Academy, Ayr

Untitled

The last thing I remember is going down a dark, muddy road with a lot of potholes, with the car bouncing up and down like a kangaroo. It was creepy because of all the thunder and lightning in the background and there were only two of us in the car: my friend Thomas and me. Thomas heard a weird noise coming from the forest beside us. Then we got to a steep hill and the car broke down. We decided to look for shelter for the night and sticks to make a fire. Then we saw a spooky cave...

Adam Phillips (12)
Ayr Academy, Ayr

The Basement

The sound was almost like a growl; low and deep, eerily familiar. I was trembling in fear, quivering with dread, so I went downstairs to the basement. I knew I had to face it alone. There was nothing to be seen but I still heard the sound and then a flash flew by me, but I couldn't catch it all, just a blur. Behind me a shadow lurked in the air, the shape of a forgotten ghost. I stupidly thought it would never come back for me but here it was. It had returned and I was its next victim.

Reece Paul Cochrane (13)
Ayr Academy, Ayr

Lily's Story

I quickly and quietly ran over to the top of the stairs. I looked down but there was no one there and no sound anywhere, except from my cat. I went down and looked around but there was no one. The TV was on but it had no signal, was making a fuzzy sound and it was black and white. I heard something behind me, I thought it was just my cat at first but then I heard my name being quietly said, so I turned around and I saw two humongous shadows behind me...

Lily Wood (12)
Ayr Academy, Ayr

The Path

The last thing I remember was that I was in the woods with my brother and we were walking along the path. I asked him a question but he was gone. I screamed, "Alex! Alex! Are you there?" But no one answered. My face was in shock. I didn't know what to do but then I saw a guy staring at me. I started to panic then started to run. I looked behind. He started to storm towards me and I sprinted like the wind. I started to think I was safe but I tripped...

Saul George Manson Stenson (11)
Ayr Academy, Ayr

Untitled

I prise open the door and watch the darkness flood towards me. *Deep breath.* The wooden steps creak beneath my feet as I descend into the basement. It's freezing. Moss clambers up the walls, fleeing from whatever horrors lie below. I have to keep going. At the bottom, the sound of clanging metal rattles round the room. I fumble with the light switch until the naked bulk in the centre of the room flickers to life. I catch a glimpse of the empty wire cage. *Wham.* Everything goes black. When I wake up, the cage is no longer empty...

Ania Bowie (15)
Fraserburgh Academy, Fraserburgh

The Mysterious Noise?

There was a noise coming from the basement and I was in my bed, so I got out very quietly. I decided to go to the basement door. To be clear, I'm not unfamiliar with the horror franchise, so instead of going inside the basement, I threw something down the stairs and bats flew out. I called the exterminator and went back to bed... but then I awoke to find that it was just a bad dream. I was glad I didn't have to pay a ridiculous amount of money, or disturb those bats!

Tegan Davidson (15)
Fraserburgh Academy, Fraserburgh

My Vision?

That was it, it was gone. My childhood and everything I ever loved. "Why? Why would you do this to me?" I cried out, hoping for an answer.

"Why do you think?" a deep voice asked. I froze in fear. My beautiful Earth was completely destroyed. "You're special."

"No, I'm not," I shouted. "Maybe I am..." I muttered to myself.

"You see, you can see things! You had the vision."

"What do you mean by *vision*?"

"If it wasn't for your dream, all humans would be dead."

"What is the point of two humans?" I asked.

"Oh. You'll see..."

Rachel Macdonald (11)
Grangemouth High School, Grangemouth

Myth

"The last thing I remember is burning and screaming, so I ran and that's how I got here, the middle of nowhere."
"Please tell us more!"
"Okay." There was a long pause.
"The town was on fire, falling apart. People not understanding what was going on. But I'm sure I heard roaring."
"From a lion or-?" Suddenly, there was a loud noise as a tall boy crashed into the room.
"No! She heard a dragon! It's destroying the city with other mythical creatures! We need to find the magical book, the only thing that can save us from the myth!"

Emily Ann Reid (12)
Grangemouth High School, Grangemouth

The Freaks

They're back. Again. I can remember these freaks at this very tree, dancing, freaking people out. This time, scaring me. They might be aliens. They're not humans, definitely not. When I got in, I asked my parents to see what they thought. They just told me to go and rest for a bit. When I went back, they weren't there, so I started walking back and *bang!* They appeared. They're green, have massive heads, three eyes, four legs and eight arms. They looked so intimidating, it was unreal. They chased me, running faster and faster. They had me trapped... Noo!

Nathan Baird (12)
Grangemouth High School, Grangemouth

Footsteps

There is a noise coming from the basement... I run down the stairs and I hear loud breathing. The door closes. I hear footsteps getting louder and louder, getting closer and closer. I hear someone shout, "Run!" I trip over the washing machine, place my hand down, then feel something. I jump up and look... It's a child's bones! When I run to open the door, it's completely locked but that door isn't supposed to lock... ever! The footsteps start again. This time, it's stomps that get louder and louder. The floor starts to fall apart and... "Aaahh!"

Kyraa Murray (12)
Grangemouth High School, Grangemouth

Save Me!

At birth, everyone's tattooed with their date of death. Mine's dated yesterday. My friend Sally wasn't due until five years tomorrow. She died yesterday. Something scary is happening. My cousin Sam, his death wasn't supposed to happen until next May. It's January 2043. I saw them both yesterday before they died. I also saw my former friend, Maria. I hugged her when she left. Now she's dead too. I think there is something wrong with me. If I touch someone, they die on my death date! Please, please help me and save me from this!

Tegan Berry (12)
Grangemouth High School, Grangemouth

Test 317

"She is awake, start test 317," I heard the scientist say. I must have lost consciousness. I remember running down an old abandoned street, being chased, so I banged on the door.

It swung open. Without hesitation, I rushed inside. I remember seeing a man in a white suit. He frantically grabbed me, but why? Will I ever see my loving mum and stuck-up dad again?

My heart was beating as loud as a drum, faster and faster. Suddenly, I felt electricity rush through my bones. It hurt.

"Please don't take my superpowers!"

How did they find out?

Brooke Morrison (12)
Grangemouth High School, Grangemouth

The Creak

There is a high-pitched noise coming from the basement. I'm used to creaks and groans from the old floorboards but this is different. Intrigued by this, I fetch a candle and head for the rusty basement door. My stomach churns. I open the door to nothing but forbidding darkness. Should I ignore it? No. Taking one step at a time, I slowly descend the stairs, my heart thumping vigorously. The candlelight flickers as an eerie breath of wind passes by. I hear it again. It's louder. I'm rooted to the spot but I know it's behind me...

Greer Hunter (12)
Grangemouth High School, Grangemouth

The Light

At birth, everyone's tattooed with their date of death. Mine's dated yesterday. Was I still alive or was I dreaming? It was real life. I wondered, *If I was meant to die yesterday, why am I still alive?* Everything rushed through my head. Everyone I knew had died, or were going to, because they were born around the same time as me. No family. No one cared about me. I shouldn't be here, I should be dead. Then everything felt fine, no worries at all. I felt weightless. I looked up and I saw a bright light... Then I realised.

Lucy Rebecca Kemp (12)
Grangemouth High School, Grangemouth

Family Or Not?

I unravel the family portrait; if these are my parents, who's that downstairs? Am I adopted? Where are my parents? I have lived with these people my whole life, or have I? These people could be strangers and the kids that I call my brothers, are they strangers? These people on the portrait look so different. Did they dye their hair? What should I do, stay here or run? Run where though...? I don't have contact with anyone. Wait... That's why they're not my real family!

Weeks after, I found out I was kidnapped when I was little!

Kate Temporal (12)
Grangemouth High School, Grangemouth

Once Upon A Death

I unravel the family portrait; if these are my parents, who's that downstairs? I just stood there, frozen in fear, then I heard a noise. *Creak, creak, creak.* Someone was watching me. I was so scared. I didn't know what to do. It had been five minutes and I was still holding the portrait. I turned around and nobody was there, so I slowly but curiously walked towards the stairwell. The wooden stairs creaked. I was so loud! One more step...

"Two days ago, a girl called Emma was killed. Her death is unexplained."

Claire Helen Campbell (11)
Grangemouth High School, Grangemouth

The Last Ride

The last thing I remember is going on a ride in the woods with my favourite horse, Valentino and now I am lying in a hospital bed. I can sort of remember seeing someone or something, but it was a blur. Anyway, what happened in the woods, I don't know. I've been told by doctors I have been shot. I ask about my horse. They say he's nowhere to be seen. I am scared. What happened? Where is my horse? Who shot me?

Beep, beep, beep...

The machine flatlined.

"She is dead, and she was only sixteen..."

Mia Sarah Hamilton (12)
Grangemouth High School, Grangemouth

5am

I could remember waking up that morning, but I couldn't remember falling asleep. I woke up at 5am, still tired. I heard a noise coming from the basement. Carefully, I tried to wake up Mum and Dad. They didn't budge. Silently, I slid down the banister to avoid the creak of the wooden stairs. I opened the door to our basement. I started to look around. There was nothing too suspicious, except a weird-looking door in the corner. Did I dare to enter? Then I woke up Mum and Dad.
They said, "You're being silly, back to bed..."

Katie Fraser (12)
Grangemouth High School, Grangemouth

Dream Saga

As I awake I wonder, *Where am I?* The sky's not blue and the grass isn't green. They're completely opposite. Am I upside down or is this place upside down? There are no words to describe it. There's nothing around me apart from the grass and the sky. It's like I'm in a weird video game, where no matter how far you look, it's just all the same... Except this thing coming towards me. It's like some sort of shadow. There are no words to describe its shape, it's taking the words out of my mouth. What do I do?

Kayleigh Mitchell (12)
Grangemouth High School, Grangemouth

I Am The Wolf

Wolves howl in the background. They're wounded, filled with pain. It was abandoned by its pack. I know what the wolf feels - the despair of being abandoned. I limped from the dead, hearing a growl near me. In the bushes, a wolf growled but I didn't feel fear. I am the wolf. As the night moon shone, the bite mark on my face seared like before, when first inflicted. My body burned, my blood raced. I lifted my hand like I've done so many times before. Fur burst through my skin; bones grew, changed form. I am the wolf.

Callum Xander McGarry (12)
Grangemouth High School, Grangemouth

Science Lab Virus

In the science lab, we found a letter and a plastic bag. We opened the letter and read it. It read, 'I need to tell someone, before it's too late. Yours sincerely, Dr Brown'. We opened the plastic bag, and a virus spread around the lab, then outside. The virus alarm went off and we'd all passed out after five minutes.

After ten minutes, we all woke up. We turned the TV on and switched to the news channel. There was an announcement that a virus had been released. People were getting infected and we were all terrified...

Aiden Andrew Keltie (11)
Grangemouth High School, Grangemouth

The Story Of Exe

My friend was inside the land with the red sky and outside was the electrical fence. There was a sign that said *Keep Out. Dangerous Monster!* Me and my two friends didn't care, we just wanted to see our friend.

The gate opened by itself. By the time we went in, there was blood everywhere. I touched his shoulder. He looked at me, then his eyes turned red and black. He said, "I am God!"

He killed my friends. I got out of that place. I thought, *I need to tell someone before it's too late!*...

Da'ud Murtaza (12)
Grangemouth High School, Grangemouth

Lucky Ones

At birth, everyone's tattooed with their date of death. Mine's dated yesterday. I woke up. It hit me. "I should be dead!" I felt pathetic, like a turtle retreating to its shell. People normally think I'm retentive but I couldn't remember a thing from the day before. As I went to see the doctor about this, someone pulled me into an alley. As they covered my mouth, they also pulled me to a white facility with big writing: 'Lucky Ones'. It gave me a chill down my spine. As he threw me down, I was scared for my life...

Ethan John Murray (12)
Grangemouth High School, Grangemouth

It Can't Be!

I got off the plane. The terminal was empty. There must be something wrong, I was meant to meet my mum. Where is she? I need to find her. What have I missed? What year is it? Oh no, I have been away for so long, sixty-four years I think! Wait, where is my phone? I can't believe it, why did I freeze for so long? I should have been away for ten!

Who is that? Wait, "Father, is that really you? It can't be, you died years ago!"

"No son, you died years ago."

"What! No. No. No!"

Regan Galletly (12)
Grangemouth High School, Grangemouth

The Nightmare

I got off the plane, the terminal was empty. No one was at border control. I would have waited hours on end usually. I went to baggage reclaim. I was desperate to urinate. As I ran into the toilet, I heard a noise, a growling one. I took a few steps backwards, then something touched my shoulders. That's when I fell. I woke up covered in blood, from my forehead down to my toenails. I was surrounded by crocodiles, men with guns, lions, tigers, polar bears and pandas. They began to charge. The men began to shoot at me! RIP.

Ben Keenan (11)
Grangemouth High School, Grangemouth

Lift-Off

Every single rock propelled me up and down. I felt tickles of the air as it rushed below my nervously trembling feet. Like soldiers on the back of frozen arms, hair stood up. *Why is no one here?* rushed through me, through every corner. It was quiet, not a single peep, not a single driver upgrading me. Suddenly, I was thrust back into my seat, the roar of an engine propelled a hunk of cracking metal faster and faster. The rocks below me forced me up and down. Then a violent rock made me see the Earth disappear...

William Lawless (12)
Grangemouth High School, Grangemouth

Gunshots

There was a noise coming from the basement. It was loud. A gunshot? I jumped. I didn't expect it. I wondered what it was. I was the only person in the house. Wasn't I? I eventually gathered the strength and courage to get up out of bed. I opened my bedroom door as slowly as possible, hoping it would not squeak. I slowly tiptoed down both sets of stairs, hoping the floorboards wouldn't squeak. I went into the dark basement. No one was there. Nothing had moved. As I stepped into the basement, I could make out fast movements...

Cameron Dougall (12)
Grangemouth High School, Grangemouth

The Mystery Person

I have Max with me. Everything feels weird, but the same. I am petrified. I hate this. I go up to the weird attic, quietly. I don't want them to hear me. Suddenly, I find a portrait which I unravel. If these are my parents, who's that downstairs? We walk downstairs quietly. We look over the banister, and we see a policeman. What is he doing? Where are they? This is bad... We have to run away. I reach for the door, but it's locked. "What's going on?" I say. Then I see what was downstairs...

Olivia Stewart (11)
Grangemouth High School, Grangemouth

I Tried To Tell You, I Tried To Stop Death

I need to tell someone the truth, before it's too late. I slammed the door. I got on my bike as the rain bounced off the road. When I got to his house, I saw him in the window, not moving. The door was wide open. As I stepped in, he still didn't move. I placed my hand on his hard shoulder. The dummy fell apart. My brain told me to stop. I looked up at a hole in the roof, there he was.

"Goodbye," he said.

Slam. I'm now locked inside because I didn't listen to my brain...

Connor Davey (12)
Grangemouth High School, Grangemouth

Strangers

I unravel the family portrait; if these were my parents, who are the people that are downstairs? Two strangers had been looking after me! There was banging noises coming from the basement... I opened the door and there was two shivering people tied up with rope. A man and a woman but they didn't look like the people in the portrait. In fact, it looked like my aunt and uncle that I hadn't seen in ages. I knew I had to get out of that house but when I got to the top stair, the door had gone...

Madison MacDonald (12)
Grangemouth High School, Grangemouth

The Abandoned Airport

I get off the plane. The terminal is empty. The cold, damp floor makes my shoes squelch with every step I take. It is dark and eerie with broken walls, chairs and tables. The only light I can see is the one coming from a 'staff only' base. The only noise I hear is the sound of my shoes as I slowly creep towards the suspicious light, beyond the 'staff only' door. Suddenly, I hear a gunshot coming from the base and the staffroom light dies with the sound of male and female screams...

Roan Buckham (12)
Grangemouth High School, Grangemouth

The Hospital

At birth, everyone's tattooed with their date of death. Mine's dated yesterday. The cold air hits my face as I run out of the hospital. Why did they take me? What do they want with my blood? My head throbs as my feet hit the ground. I am so weak but I have to keep running. The lack of sleep is showing. Men in white chase after me and the gap between us is closing now. The last thing I remember is my mum shouting my name and crying. She was a blubbering mess. Everything falls black and very quiet...

Charlotte Makin (12)
Grangemouth High School, Grangemouth

Alone And Scared!

The last thing I remember is that morning I was going to the haunted town Mum told me never to set foot in. I remember walking in slowly, with slight hesitation. It was a grim, dull place. Straight away, I remember my heart pounding and my mouth becoming bone dry, almost as if I knew something was going to happen. I was right. I heard a loud, echoing siren. I felt alone and scared and now I was lying there, frightened. My mind was frantically wondering where I was. What was going on? Where was my mum?

Lauren Kirkham (12)
Grangemouth High School, Grangemouth

The Thing

I awoke to a blurred vision. Someone was in my room. I hauled my covers over in bewilderment. I peered out, something was there. I took a whiff of air in to see if I could sniff something out. As I peeked out, I got a glimpse of it. It was like an immaterial substance. I robbed another look; it was unfolding in front of me. It started to come closer. I tried to scream the house down but nothing came out. Then it started to come towards me. *Beep! Beep! Beep!* I awoke to my alarm!

Gregor Hunter (12)
Grangemouth High School, Grangemouth

A Place I Want To Be

Today was the fifteenth day since I ran away. I didn't want to be put in any 'category'. I'm not smart, brave, helpful or selfless. I'm going somewhere where people have no categories. You spend time on you. Some say it's not true. My dad sent letters from far away, about how he was and always asked if I was okay, but Mum didn't want me to reply. I believe my dad. I don't know if I should. He said that I should meet him there. I hope I will meet him there...

Ashly Kidd (11)
Grangemouth High School, Grangemouth

Trapped

There was a noise coming from the basement, something was watching me. I tried to move my arms but they felt chained up. My mouth was open but I couldn't say a word. I tried to scream but it was no use, my mouth was gagged. My arms were getting looser and I managed to break free and run.

I was outside but I knew if I stopped, I would be caught. When I thought it was safe, I stopped, but as soon as I did, I got knocked out! It was dragging me, dragging me back to my doom!...

Lottie Tyler Mears (12)
Grangemouth High School, Grangemouth

Untitled

There was a noise coming from the basement. *Creak, creak, creak*. As I walked closer to the basement, I could hear that the noise was coming from the floorboards, like someone was creeping up to the basement door. I took small steps to the door, hoping it was just Mum washing out clothes, but it wasn't promising. I slowly opened the door. Something moved. That's when I saw it. It wasn't a person, nor an animal. The thing came closer to me. I screamed!

Carla Shaw (12)
Grangemouth High School, Grangemouth

The Unknown Myth

We watched from the space station as Earth exploded. It felt as if we were watching it in slow motion. My heart thumped like it was going to jump out of my chest and break in two. All those innocent people should still be here! All those myths became true right in front our eyes and only ten of us got to live. They still had a life to live and things to see but everything is gone! Life won't be the same even for us... It should have been me!

Amber Wilson (11)
Grangemouth High School, Grangemouth

The Date Of Death

At birth, everyone's tattooed with their date of death. Mine's dated yesterday. I am still alive. Why am I still alive? I really don't understand. I feel very scared but nervous at the same time because if I didn't die yesterday, when *will* I die? Everyone else I know has died on their dates. I wonder if they have forgotten? I hear a noise... They are coming! No... Am I doing to die? What will I do? Hide!

Nicole Davidson (12)
Grangemouth High School, Grangemouth

The Observer

Somebody other than me needs to know the truth. That I was there that night. I saw it all. The way he tricked her. It was all an act. She soon realised and she fought back. He took a knife to her neck and stabbed it. She laid there and screamed and shrieked and bled. They called from downstairs but he said he was busy. I guess he was. I still love him because he is my dad, but I miss her because she was my mother.

Angus Tulloch (12)
Grangemouth High School, Grangemouth

No-Man's-Land

The last thing I remember is Tim leaving the town looking for supplies, but he didn't come back. We looked for three weeks but there was nothing.

One day, we were in an abandoned city and we came across some raiders. We killed all of them, and then the leader of the raiders opened a door and Tim came out. He was different because the raiders had brainwashed him. The leader got the jump on me, and told Tim to kill me. Tim shot the leader and broke down in tears. I held him and said, "It's okay."

Kieran Loughhead (13)
Inverness High School, Inverness

A Past Life

The last thing I remember is being dragged along by my old friends. Everyone tells me I'm making it up, it's a dream. It isn't true. I do know that I used to be a different person, I remember it.

I used to be in the army. I have memories of World War Two, I had a friend, John Mitchell, I was at his funeral about eighty years ago.

Whenever I tell anyone, they say, "You're only twenty-one tomorrow." I will fly to my old home in Germany and prove it to them!

Paige Morrison (14)

Inverness High School, Inverness

Detective

The last thing I remember was seeing a blur. I woke up at my desk, unable to remember anything from last night. Detective Jones pounded at my door.

"Dylan, we have a murder case. Let's get to the scene in Glasgow!"

As he drove me, the industrial surroundings looked familiar, but I didn't know why. When we arrived, I saw the weapon. A knife. I instantly spotted a CCTV camera on the wall.

"A camera!"

After I arrived at the control centre, I searched the footage. The murderer looked straight at the camera. I saw my face. Now I remember...

Dylan McCabe (15)
Lenzie Academy, Lenzie

The Cure Is Near

I need to tell someone the truth before it's too late. I've been in the camp for ten days now and the things outside the walls are groaning louder every day. I hear the occasional gunshot at night. *Bang!*

Ring! That was the emergency alarm. They've broken through the walls! I have been working on this cure for the last few weeks, but it's packed up in boxes, ready to be shipped. *Crash!* The doors are down. If anybody finds this report, you need to use the vaccine against them... but help me first!

Aiden Glasswell (14)

Lenzie Academy, Lenzie

Moonlight

The sun was blazing through the mist. He took out the map, searching for a clue. He paced back and forth, turning over every rock and stone. The sun was setting. He looked out across the valley. A vast land with no wildlife, no plants. Empty. *I must be missing something,* he thought. He said down on a pale, grey rock and looked through his bag. "Key, check. Map, check. What could it be?"
The moon rose and pierced the clouds, hitting the cliff side and cracking it. He jumped off the rock, The moonlight revealed a keyhole...

Aaron Wilkie (14)
Lenzie Academy, Lenzie

The Empty Terminal

I got off the plane. The terminal was empty. I was looking to see why on earth no one was here. Suddenly, I heard screaming in the distance. I kept my breath steady and flexed my fingers, then started walking towards it.
That's when I saw it.
Something I wish I'd never seen: a small, deformed, demonic figure. I could hear it making painful groaning noises. As I snuck away, I heard footsteps behind me, as though the weird creature was following me everywhere I went. He got faster and faster. Then he was gone. Or so I thought...

Jack Cullen (15)
Lenzie Academy, Lenzie

My Final Hours

My final hours. Everyone is born with a twenty-year timer.
You work to gain more time, and my time is about to expire.
I tried my hardest to find work, but it was no use. One
hour and forty-five minutes and counting. No one is going to
save me now. Well, all that's left to do now is sit here in this
small, dark room, waiting for the moment that everyone
dreads, when the clock says zero. So here I am, writing this,
twenty seconds before I die.
Five, four, three, two, one, zero...
"What? I'm still alive!"

Sean Bill McLaughlin (15)
Lenzie Academy, Lenzie

End Of The World!

We looked back at Earth as the moon collided with the planet. We had five seconds to get away from the explosion, so we wouldn't get hit by the blast. We jetted out quick enough, but I wondered to myself with worry what we'd do if the oxygen ran out in our supply. We couldn't go back to get more, and what would we do if the food supplies ran out? As we flew away from Earth, I heard a bang on the spaceship. A hole appeared in the wall. We were going to die...

Robbie Andrew Goodfellow (15)
Lenzie Academy, Lenzie

Start Over

Theres something truly beautiful about absolute destruction. When not a thing is left behind. The world was becoming immeasurably hostile. Violence caused by the ignorance of many. The Earth and its beauty was completely unappreciated, so I took it away from them. Years of planning all came down to this. Five hundred people, carefully chosen. We'll start over. A new civilisation. I will prevent this from happening again. Two years up here and Mars will be fully habitable. I will create a pure society. I cannot stop until this is perfect. I need to show that I've changed...

Heather Amy Needham (15)
Queen Margaret Academy, Ayr

An Ancient Tomb

The sun was blazing down. I took out the map, the tomb was nearby. As I walked through the scorching desert, I saw a path. Was it a mirage or not? I followed it. *Incredible*, I thought. It was the tomb. I heard a scream followed by a roar from the inside. Outside the tomb, there was a sign. It read, *Here Lays The Legendary*. I went inside. The first thing I saw were the bodies of bandits. I immediately took cover, but I was too late. I saw him. He has awakened. The legendary Blue Eyes White Dragon...

Kaloyan Galev (15)
Queen Margaret Academy, Ayr

Mine

The darkness engulfed me in an instant. The satisfaction of completing my task filled me with excitement. Gone. Everything gone. Not one soul left. I now had an empty canvas. A world just waiting to be created in my image. My likeness. Mine. For the first time, I tasted what it was like to have true power. Nothing and no one could stop me. I was free from the chains of family, fear and death. I am an omnipotent being to rule above all. My new people will be perfect, created for one true purpose. To make the galaxy mine.

Benjamin Cochrane (15)
Queen Margaret Academy, Ayr

A Day To Die

Everyone has a day to die, but dates can be changed.
December 13th 2073, that's mine. Yet today is the
14th... *Ding dong!* My friend, Michael.
"We're going out, remember?"
"Oh," I say, remembering.
We're driving along. Michael suddenly jolts the car to a halt.
He grabs me abruptly.
"You should have died yesterday!" He yells through gritted
teeth. "Don't worry, you'll die today..."
He grabs a dagger from his pocket, and holds it high above
my head. Then I realise it is the 14th. Michael drops dead.
Everyone has a day to die...

Hattie Eleanor Fowler (11)
St George's School For Girls, Edinburgh

Run... Now...

Drip... drip...
Well, this isn't the welcome I was expecting! The plane terminal is utterly deserted. Not even a tumbleweed. What am I supposed to do? No security guy, no porters? I'm completely on my own.
Bzzz.
There's a hum of electricity in the air. Footsteps. I turn around. Nobody. The lights suddenly become so bright, I fall to the ground. I roll over, groaning.
Footsteps, again. Metal on metal.
"Well, hello there Emma. Nice to see you," a snarling voice says. No matter how bright it is, I have to get out of here, I have to run. Now...

Isla Macfadyen (11)
St George's School For Girls, Edinburgh

Untitled

Bang!
There goes the starting gun, I thought nervously, as I sprinted forward. *Remember,* I told myself, *you are simply just another kid running frantically through a hay bale maze, trying to win a spot in Labiatum, the most prestigious spy school in the universe. Right, so left or right? Well, my map says right, so there you go. You have your answer,* I think, wandering absent-mindedly into a wall. That's odd, my map says that it is this way. I turn around and notice something strange. I look and gasp. There, slightly crumbled, is my real map...

Heidi Masters (11)
St George's School For Girls, Edinburgh

Break Free

We marched in perfect synchronisation across the infinite concrete space in utter silence.

"Clear your mind," a voice broke the silence. I moved my head a tiny amount. The same uniforms, the same blank faces.

"Don't move!" Was it anger, hunger or thirst? I hadn't eaten in days. Dare I escape? Would it work? The tension built up. Three, two, one. I ran for it. Immediately, sirens wailed and a light scanned the darkness. I could feel thousands of guns pointing at me. I kept running without looking back. So, this is what it felt like to be free...

Iona Talbot Rice (11)
St George's School For Girls, Edinburgh

Being Released

London's population is constantly growing. Boston's is constantly dropping. Every day, two people get taken away. No one knows where they go, only they don't come back. There's no warning either. They just come one day and take you. I should know, because I've been taken. They don't kill you, they make you fight for your place. If you survive, they take you back to Boston. No one's ever come back though. Well, at least not in one piece. I'm on my third day of fighting. My brother came here too, and survived. Only he hasn't been released, yet...

Clara Anna Elisabeth Ahnert (11)
St George's School For Girls, Edinburgh

Her Life In A Nutshell

A dead nutshell, motionless. Ah yes, that was my sister. The most talented girl, dead. Dead because of me, Betty Grangy. My old pal wrote a letter forty-eight hours ago, asking the president to kill her, but I was the murderer as I'd told him about her tattoo. How it was out of date. They were meant to explode and kill us. It wasn't fair though, it was because I'd passed some cursed test. Her little mind was too young, too problematic, too scared. It was my fault, she could've lived. She could've learned. She could've lived life, unlike me.

Charlotte Earl (11)
St George's School For Girls, Edinburgh

Memories

Everyone's tattooed with their date of death. Mine's dated yesterday. My tattoo's not hard to see since it's on my forehead. Wait! The numbers were changing... The date was going backwards. Slowly, the days, then months. Once the years started to count back, I started to remember things. They were like memories, but... not mine. For instance, a barbecue. That seemed okay for a normal person, but not for me since I have no family. The date kept on moving closer to my date of birth. These 'memories' kept on going until it reached my date of birth... blank.

Zainab Shahid Hafeez (11)
St George's School For Girls, Edinburgh

The Terror That Awaits Me

One cold night, I went to the attic to get the family portrait. I had just had dinner with my parents. The attic was a dark, scary place with moth-eaten chairs, and dusty boxes. I turned on the light. It flickered and went out, so I grabbed a torch and I searched through the boxes and found the family portrait. I unravelled the family portrait. *If these are my parents, who's that downstairs?* I thought in horror. Downstairs, my 'parents' had changed into terrifying monsters. They lunged at me and that was the last thing I remember...

Rona Marshall (11)
St George's School For Girls, Edinburgh

Journey To Earth

The sun was blazing, I took out the map, I must be close.
The rocket was supposed to be fireproof, but flares
sometimes hit. The water supply was becoming low. I was
supposed to arrive a while ago. My trip back to Earth seems
to take longer. The stars are shimmering in the sky. The fuel
stopped. Suddenly, I was floating in space, therefore I was
stranded in space, with no communications or food. I finally
reached the atmosphere, hurtling to civilisation. The
parachute failed. It was a crash-landing. All I remembered
was waking up in the hospital. I'd survived.

Maira Lakshmy Ratnarajah (11)
St George's School For Girls, Edinburgh

The Empty Place

I found myself nervously waking up in a dark, isolated alleyway. It was pitch-black, except you could see little blood drops everywhere, and a dirty, silver nail sticking out of a destroyed door. I then slowly put down my first foot forward, and carefully waited for a sound. Unexpectedly, I heard a quiet voice from behind me, and dashed up the dark alleyway. I wanted to stop, but I couldn't stop running. It was like it would never end, like the Great Wall of China. I finally stopped, but what was the dark shadowy figure approaching me from behind?

Kate Green (11)
St George's School For Girls, Edinburgh

The Portrait

I peeked around the door to check nobody was coming, then sat in front of this huge painting in utter horror and began to wonder all the possibilities of my life, before I could remember anything. I thought quickly, and dragged the huge painting down the stairs, to show whom I thought were my parents. I walked into the room where they sat watching Countryfile and as soon as they saw me, their mouths dropped. I'd never suspected anything about my parents, but now I knew and nobody would believe the series of unfortunate events that happened next...

Eliza Gardiner (11)
St George's School For Girls, Edinburgh

Am I Dead?

When my mum found out I wasn't actually dead, she rushed me to hospital. This is what the doctor did. He took a sample of my blood, a photo of my 'death date'. Then he asked me questions like, "How old are you?" For your information, I am twelve. These are the results...
I'm fine now. According to my doctor, my tattoo has been a silly dud print. Sadly though, I shall never know when I will die. It may be today, it may be tomorrow or maybe even in sixty years! I will never know until it actually happens.

Isabella Grahamslaw (11)
St George's School For Girls, Edinburgh

Untitled

Walking back from the town hall, the flood lights were on, everybody was in their homes, waiting... and then the radio blurted and crackled as he spoke. My mother was holding my hand tight. I could hear my mother's heartbeat getting faster, as the grumpy old man spoke. Finally, the radio cracked and turned off. My mother led me by the hand downstairs to the basement. She was crying and she said to me, "I love you, I always will, now stay here..."
She ran back upstairs, and then I heard it. My mother, screaming and crying...

Honor Simpson (11)
St George's School For Girls, Edinburgh

Untitled

What is it? I slowly start walking down the creaky stairs. As I reach the basement door, I pause and think about what I'm about to do. I go in, it's dark. I reach for the lights but jump because there's something moving. *It's only a mouse,* I tell myself. As I keep on walking, I fear the worse, maybe it's a burglar or the monster that used to live under my bed. I'm still searching for the light. I stumble upon it. *I have had a good life,* I say to myself. I flick the switch on...

Chloe Taylor (11)
St George's School For Girls, Edinburgh

Fire Doesn't Just Hurt Your Skin

There was a house fire on 1st April. No one knows how it happened, until now. It was time I told someone my secret, before it was too late. Today was the day, but who should I tell? After long consideration, I decided to tell my best friend. I saw her in school and ran after her in the empty hallway. She stopped to talk and I started crying, eventually I stopped. She asked me what was wrong, and I hesitantly whispered in her right ear. After that, all I could say was, "I started the house fire..."

Orla McKenzie Gray (11)
St George's School For Girls, Edinburgh

A Picturesque Drive

Where is everyone? I think to myself as I drive along the motorway. When I press the button for the radio, no noise projects back. It must be broken or something. As I look up into the empty, clear afternoon sky, I expect to see birds, but no, nothing, no birds, no planes. Then I notice there is no sway in the trees at all. I feel as though I'm driving through a photograph. Will I suddenly hit the frame? Do I carry on driving? Do I go back home? Would I get back home? I do not know...

Rosie Simpson (11)
St George's School For Girls, Edinburgh

What Is Underneath?

I heard a noise from the basement. The noise was a low grumbling sound with occasional roaring. It was quite scary. Okay, really scary. I didn't want to go down to the basement, but temptation to go down was unbearable. I made a very stupid mistake to go down there. Now, the events that happened are scarred on me for life. I lost so many things that day, all because I woke the beast. I should've left the thing alone and it wouldn't have caused this much damage. All my fault. All I do is watch...

Anaysa Kaddeer (11)
St George's School For Girls, Edinburgh

The Weird Noise

There was a weird noise coming from the basement, I decided to go and see what it was. When I got to the stairs, my hands started shaking. I went down the stairs, each one creaking under my feet. I felt something on my shoulder. I got a big fright, but it was just a spider. I heard the noise again, I carried on walking down. I felt something brush against my skin. I found the light switch and when I turned it on, I saw that it was my cat, Pickles, dead, hanging by a rope from the rafters...

Lois Norrie (11)
St George's School For Girls, Edinburgh

The Mystical Garden

The last thing I remembered was falling into a hole. I got up and found myself in a green and peaceful garden with lots of flowers. I was walking through the garden. Suddenly, I stepped on something and noticed it was a shiny, gold key. I picked it up and found a keyhole in the bushes. I put the key in and twisted it. When I went in, all I could see was fairies. They were small and very nice and caring. They said they could grant wishes. I was amazed! Every day since then, I went to see them...

Sara Qayyum (11)
St George's School For Girls, Edinburgh

Dragons' Den

According to the map, a dragons' den was just over the hill. The air was crisp and lifeless. As I walked on, my cane rattled in my shaky hand. A rabbit ran past. How? This was a sign, a sign of life. Dragons' Den really was close. I could feel it. The smell of smoke stinging my nose. The crying sound of the wind. That was when I saw it, the mouth of the cave. I was finally here, finally at Dragons' Den...

Arabella Simpson (11)
St George's School For Girls, Edinburgh

Society

2065.
Society's only entertainment? Well, you'll see. Last thing I remember was a bright white flash, then a monstrous audience appeared before me.
"With the last person in, we can begin the show!"
The audience roared.
"First, demand for Wade!" That was me! This was my moment.
"Cut off your hand." The audience went wild, like savages. The presenter brought over a meat cleaver. I hesitate, is it worth popularity? It's all I'd ever wanted! I proceed. Blood splats against my face as I slam the knife through my wrist. The audience goes crazy, I feel pain...

Aadam Saafi (14)
Stewarton Academy, Stewarton

Reset

I wake up to silence. It's always like this. It's odd. Noise started trickling in at exactly 8am. Quiet, getting louder. I check the date. Same as yesterdays, which worries me. I step outside, joined on the way to work by neighbours and colleagues. Everyone is robotic. Calculated. Controlled, you could say. It's been this way for months. Things are strange these days. There's no individuality. No little things that make a person stand out. Too scared. There are... consequences. Suddenly, the world stops, turning into ones and zeros for just a second. I have to tell before - reset.

Anna Sinclair (13)
Stewarton Academy, Stewarton

Twins...

Auschwitz, 1942.
I'm awoken by the harrowing screams of those being murdered. Alone with my twin sister, the last thing I remember is being transported in trains which were so tightly packed that the dead were still standing. I recall the utter terror of arriving at the camp and trampling on dead people like steps as we left the train. A doctor walks in, grabs my sister and leaves. She comes back crying, bloodied and pin-pricked from injections. She's tougher than me. I'm next... He turns towards me and I look at my sister for possibly the last time.

Andrew Lancaster (14)
Stewarton Academy, Stewarton

Ignorance

Since I was conceived, I have been ignored. People walked by me every day, without any care for how I felt. For days, I sat alone with fleeting glimpses of my masters. Not even a sideways glance was cast at me, they don't care for me, not one bit. I have started to smell, but they don't seem to notice. Slowly, I feel myself withering. Days I waited to be accepted. Still, nothing. They'd forgotten me. I see the knife. Finally, someone approached. They picked me up, the last thing I remembered was being cast aside, my insides spilling out.

Matthew Lyon (14)
Stewarton Academy, Stewarton

Goodbye

Each night, I dream of a figure at the end of my hall and each night, it takes a step towards me. Last night, it was at my door. The last thing I remember is it staring down at me, but something's wrong. If I'm dead, why does it feel like I'm alive?

"Goodbye," the figure whispers as it turns around and disappears into nothingness. I awake to hear a sobbing sound. I walk towards it, to find my mother crying. Each night, my gran got sicker and last night, she died. It's something I don't understand...

Max Burns (14)
Stewarton Academy, Stewarton

Peaceful, For Now

I'm watching her sleep. Peaceful. I do this most nights. Sometimes, I lay and imitate her breathing. Peaceful. I mean a lot to her, but she means nothing to me. Someday I will leave, but until then, I watch her. Peaceful. The way she holds me and I in return hold her, might make one think I love her. I don't. She opens her eyes and gives me a glance. I freeze, but still watch her. She cuddles me and turns over. Releasing her grasp, I fall onto the floor. Peaceful. I'm watching her sleep. I'm watching her sleep. Peaceful...

Orla MacDonald (14)
Stewarton Academy, Stewarton

End Of The Season

It's always been perfect here, great; the family, the house, and we seem to be paid for our mere existence. Then, one day, everything turned awry. My family tore itself apart then knitted itself together. As this all continued upstairs, a low buzzing noise started emanating from the basement. It got louder as the drama intensified, and the fights got bloodier until the drama stopped.

I stood up and as the buzzing consumed all, I heard a man proclaim, "Find out what happens to K.K next time, in a new season..."

Benjamin Michael Dalley (14)

Stewarton Academy, Stewarton

The Shadow Of A Nightmare

The last thing I could remember was lying in bed. I query about the menacing shadow made by the neighbouring trees, and the noises made by the rustling leaves. I worry the darkness will consume me when I am not looking and eat me like it did the others. That is the nightmare I have every night. I feel scared, confused and helpless. What if it succeeds in its own endeavours? I wish I could leave the nightmares behind. There is still one thing I do not understand. How can you have a nightmare if you don't fall asleep?

Rowan McClure (14)
Stewarton Academy, Stewarton

The Girl Next Door

I always thought the girl next door was strange. Every time I saw her, she was covered in cuts and bruises. The night I found out why was a night I'd never forget. I was in my bedroom, on a normal Tuesday night, when I heard a bang from next door. I thought nothing of it, until there was a young girl's scream. I saw her being punched by her stepdad. I had to tell someone, but I froze. The screams got louder and louder, then weaker and weaker until they stopped, silence.
It was too late.

Ella Duncan (14)
Stewarton Academy, Stewarton

Artificial Intelligence

As I woke up, my AI stared at me with intent. He wanted to do something, I don't know what. The last thing I remember was being escorted to the basement and being put into some sort of machine. I am very cold, where am I? I was frozen. I walked up the stairs and looked at the calendar. It was the year 2118.

101 years later, I walked outside. All I saw for miles were brainwashed humans being used for slavery, with the AI being their master. I turned swiftly, only to feel a needle going into my leg...

Grant McClure (14)
Stewarton Academy, Stewarton

Untitled

I creep up the stairs, not making a sound. As I open the door, my knife positioned in my hand, my eyes sweep the room. The terminal is empty. Good. I break out into a sprint, or as close as I can get to a sprint with my injured leg, towards the gate that will lead to the plane. The plane that will fly me away from here, away from all the killing and lying and betrayal. As I turn into the gate, a bullet punctures my heart. At least I don't have to stay here any more...

Sam Speirs (14)
Stewarton Academy, Stewarton

A Dark Room

I can remember being alone and cold, very cold. I can remember not knowing where I was, or where I would go. I can remember feeling trapped, not having a way out. I can remember not knowing alone, that someone or something was there with me. I can remember not knowing who I was, or where I came from, not even if I had a family. I can remember being scared, petrified, but I felt no pain, no suffering. I remember hearing a click, then a bright light, my eyes got used to the light...

Bryn Harzmeyer (14)
Stewarton Academy, Stewarton

Reconsideration

Holding it all in is too much. I can't let go of what happened, no matter how much I try. I remember every emotion, every touch. Kevin from work boasts about his nights out, how he loves it and how it's all part of being a man. I just want to be free from him, his power, even though I know I am. Inside me, I want to die, as if my integrity and soul has been stripped away from me and now I'm just a lifeless body. It is all too much to wish away...

Morgan Daniel Cumming (14)
Stewarton Academy, Stewarton

Granny Summerfield

I got off the plane, the terminal was empty.
"Are you Amber? Erm... I mean, hello Amber," greeted Granny Summerfield, peeking out of the corner.
"Hi Granny, how are you?" she quivered.
"I'm alright, darling." That made me suspicious. Granny never said darling.
Later, I heard sirens...
"What's going on?"
"Hide!" shrieked Granny.
Bang... There were unexpected gunshots.
"You're under arrest Mrs Green," said a police officer, positioning his gun on Granny. "It turns out, your so-called 'granny' here isn't your real granny," he said just after the arrest, "she was actually here to kidnap you..."

Bente van West (12)

The Gordon Schools, Huntly

The Secret

I need to tell someone the truth before it's too late. I sat in the living room with that same thought rushing through my head. Another thought suddenly popped into my mind. *What about the kids?* I started to feel hot and sweaty. There was sudden sharp pain in my chest. I collapsed onto the floor with a dreadful thud. My wife came in and screamed. That's all I remember. I woke in the hospital, and saw my wife crying. *Man up,* I tell myself, *you can't keep it a secret any longer.*
"I have cancer," I said, "I'm dying."

Lauren Ferguson (13)
The Gordon Schools, Huntly

Blackout

"Bella, wake up!" Sarah was violently shaking me. "It's Jimmy, he's been murdered! Hurry and meet me downstairs in five minutes, the police are interviewing everybody on the street."

With that, she quickly skidded away. I could only see faint stars and flickers of light as I tumbled out of bed, only vaguely aware that I was in yesterday's clothes. I went to the sink to brush my teeth, then gazed down at my hands. They were covered in blood. Hyperventilating, I caught a glimpse of my reflection, then it hit me. I asked myself, *Did I kill Jimmy?*

Freya Helen Tamiozzo Wilson (13)
The Gordon Schools, Huntly

The Package

The postman came. The package was addressed to me. I opened it. There was a note that read, *You're In Trouble!* It was a picture, of who I'm not sure. The little boy looked exactly like me. Was it me? Who were the two other people? Are they my mum and dad? They didn't look like that though.

I was confused, someone sent me a picture with a note that said, *You're In Trouble*. What could that possibly mean? I was at home with my family. Was I adopted? Then I heard my so-called parents say, "He can never know..."

Lucy Barclay (13)
The Gordon Schools, Huntly

Untitled

Day one, 1984.
We have just moved into our new house, perfect for a family
of four; me, Jake, my sister Lindsey, my dad Jason and my
mum, June. It is New Year tomorrow. I am really happy, and
my family can't wait for it. It is now the night before New
Year.
One year later, 1985.
"Happy New Year!" everyone shouted, as we had our
munchies. After we finished singing, which is what my family
always did on New Year. We heard a smash! Our front door
smashed. We heard a noise coming from the basement...

Callum Paterson (12)
The Gordon Schools, Huntly

The Fuse Box

The rain grew heavier as Edith cuddled into Johnnie. It was getting late, maybe about ten thirty.

"We won't be late," her mother's words rang in her ears.

Where are they? I thought they'd be home by now, Edith thought to herself. She began to feel worried. She looked at Johnnie, who had fallen asleep, snoring loudly. She switched on the TV, and the lights began to flicker.

A moment or so later, the TV began to flash. *Bang!* A fuse had gone. As Edith made her way to the fuse box, there was a knock at the door...

Laura Brown (13)
The Gordon Schools, Huntly

Collision

The last thing I remember is going in slow motion, feeling the collision as my car collides with another vehicle and the blood starts oozing down my face. My airbag fails, I feel my legs stuck in place while the car is upside down. I attempt to get out of the car. The door is prised open, then I hear movement. I stall. The crunch of the leaves comes closer. I feel someone's presence and my ears start buzzing. Next, I can't see anything, only a blur. The only thing I feel is darkness, then nothing...

Elise Desgouttes (12)
The Gordon Schools, Huntly

The Woman Downstairs

I unravelled the family portrait; if these are my parents, who's that downstairs? I snuck downstairs in my striped pyjamas and Chewbacca slippers, to find a man being interrogated by a woman. The woman, with snake-like hair and mouth like a squid's, turned her horrid head towards me.

"You're meant to be in bed!" she bellowed in a slurred voice, as if she had a mouth full of food. Her face turned into a woman again and she started to approach me. Then her face went back to her oily self, and she jumped...

Thomas Hinton (12)
The Gordon Schools, Huntly

Hospital Horror

The last thing I remember is hitting a ghostly woman and checking if she was OK. Then, when I couldn't find her, I think I passed out. I'm now in a hospital. I think everyone but me is asleep, because I can't hear anything. No footsteps, no babies crying, no nothing. The only thing that has come to my five senses is the smell, the smell is disgusting. It smells sort of like a corpse. I want to go and investigate, but I can't... I can't move. She is holding me down. She said something I couldn't understand...

Samara Irvine (11)
The Gordon Schools, Huntly

Valak Returns

There was a noise coming from the basement. I was in my house home alone. I slowly tiptoed down the creaky stairs, and saw an old man on a rocking chair. I slowly approached him, and put my hand on his shoulder. My heart stopped. He turned around. It was my mum's face on an elderly man's body. I jolted back, but I couldn't move.

I said, "Who are you?"

It replied, "I am Valak!" As it just said that, it blew into dust. I never saw Valak again, and now I am forty years old and still scared...

Scott Milne (12)
The Gordon Schools, Huntly

Screams

Why hadn't they taken me to the cliff yet? Normally, they would call your number and take you to it. A million thoughts rushed through my head. Someone said the guards had caught an illness... Screaming came from Tent 2 and I saw something purple crawl behind them. Something huge made the ground shake... I realised why there was screaming, as I caught a glimpse of it. I think it was purple. I saw something sharp too. It rammed the end of my tent, giving me enough time to run. I heard another scream, this one coming from me...

Rosa Bressers (13)
The Gordon Schools, Huntly

The Robbery

The last thing I remember was my mother's terrified face, as a bunch of burglars smashed the windows to our house. They came running through to the living room and took all of my dad's trains that he'd collected over the years. My mother was crying. She was also very fond of the trains, and she had helped collect them as well. We didn't dare move or make a noise as we could see that they were armed men with hand guns and knives. We waited till they had gone to call for help. We eventually got them arrested.

Innes Cranna (13)
The Gordon Schools, Huntly

Untitled

I unravel my family portrait; if these are parents, who's that downstairs? I head down the dark blue stairs. As they creak, I hear a noise in the basement. Stupidly, I walk down the corridor and I hear a dripping noise coming from the door to my left. On the top of the door, in gold writing, it reads, *The Basement*. I turn the handle and open the door slowly. As I take a few steps down, I feel a small drop of liquid dribbling down my face. All I remember was seeing the most horrifying sight ever...

Sam Mitchell (12)
The Gordon Schools, Huntly

Shadows

I was walking towards the front door to unlock it, just to find it was open. I walked in, bracing myself for anything. I couldn't hear or see anyone... I saw a shadow that I didn't recognise. I walked through to the living room and I heard a scream. I ran through to the kitchen, and saw a man lying on the floor with a stab wound. My sister was nearby in shock, and my brother was nowhere to be seen. I heard the tap and saw my mum with a knife, it was the same shape as the wound...

Ailie Maclennan (12)
The Gordon Schools, Huntly

The Space Station

We watched from the space station as Earth exploded. We stood in silence. All of us, too shocked to say anything. Earth had just exploded. Out homes were never to be seen again. Our families were never to be seen again. Our whole world was never to be seen again. We all just stared into nothingness, into the place where out planet should be. Suddenly, I realised we too would end up dead, like other humans. The oxygen would eventually run out. I quickly did the maths. We had twenty days left to live...

Alice Wilson (12)
The Gordon Schools, Huntly

Frozen In Fear

There was a noise coming from the basement. I didn't want to go down because it was dark, dark and spooky. As I tiptoed down the thick cement stairs and reached the bottom, I couldn't see anything. I pulled the string for the light, but it didn't work. I was frozen in fear. Then there was a sudden noise. It was like a rumble. As I took a few more steps, I heard footsteps and I saw eyes. The lights flashed, I saw it. It was a monster. He was huge with sharp teeth. I screamed and ran...

Jade Mackie (13)
The Gordon Schools, Huntly

The Last Day Of Sanity

The last thing I remember is... that night in the wood cabin. I haven't been myself since then, and I'm determined to find out what happened. I woke up next to the very old oak tree, with an extreme case of amnesia. The first thing I saw was a mysterious man running from tree to tree, wearing a black hoody. I thought I was hallucinating, so I just lay there, but then I heard a woman scream! I ran through the forest as fast as I could, but the man in the black hoody pulled me into a dark tunnel...

Rebecca Watson (11)
The Gordon Schools, Huntly

Terror Terminal

I get off the plane. The terminal is empty. I slowly creep through, I am the only person here... wait, who's that? Oh, it's just the echo of my footsteps. I walk over to one of the foot stalls. In the fridge, where the sandwiches normally are, there are hands, feet and jars of blood. I spin around as quickly as I can, and I see a man wearing a mask run towards me. He has a knife in his hand; he pushes me aggressively against the glass.
"You're next!"

Candice Lauw (12)
The Gordon Schools, Huntly

The Basement

There was a noise coming from the basement, I was curious to find out what it was. It sounded strange for an animal noise, if it was an animal. I tiptoed down the stairs because it was 1.30am. I was home alone, and I didn't want that thing to know I was coming. Then, I got a baseball bat and a torch and I opened the door as quiet as I could. I flashed my torch around the room. A black figure was hitting something and then it saw me. It started walking slowly towards me, then I hit it...

Ross MacPherson (12)
The Gordon Schools, Huntly

No Escape

The last thing I remember was clutching my parents' hands, and the screaming, there was lots of screaming. We were spinning, we were falling fast and then everything went black. The next thing I knew, I was lying on a beach, the sun glaring in my face and the water tickling my toes. I sat up, my back aching and my head throbbing. Then it occurred to me. How was I still alive? Who brought me here? There was no wreckage, nothing. I was stuck on an island by myself and no one was coming...

Rona Duncan (13)
The Gordon Schools, Huntly

Unfortunate Landings

I got off the plane and it is empty. I heard gunfire and screaming in the dark, smoky air. The stewards were telling us to get back onto the plane. I realised that a terrorist act had been committed.

"We are flying to the nearest airport. It is an hour away." Once we landed, I got off the plane and looked around, the terminal was empty. As soon as I got off the plane, it exploded. The weird thing about that was that I was the one who had detonated the bomb.

Thomas Eadon (12)
The Gordon Schools, Huntly

The Surprise

There was a noise coming from the basement. The noise
sounded like a dog growling, but my dog, Fred, was sitting
beside me. I crawled downstairs from my bedroom. Then, I
got to the basement door. I slowly opened the door, but
didn't turn on the lights, so they wouldn't know I was there. I
slowly walked down with my dog. Then, I heard the noise
again. It kept on making the same sound. Fred barked and
ran away, so I was by myself. I made it down the stairs and
saw my dad...

Lewis Murray (12)
The Gordon Schools, Huntly

The Terminal

I got off the plane, the terminal was empty. I had just got off the plane from a holiday in Italy and the place was very quiet. I didn't think anything of it, and just stared out of the window. I saw no one come on to the plane, only the one flight attendant. I looked around... nothing. Complete silence. Not a soul in sight. The flight attendant looked at me. There was no one in front of me. No one behind me. Complete silence. As I walked off the plane, I heard screaming...

Emma Buyers (12)
The Gordon Schools, Huntly

Est.1991

YOUNG WRITERS INFORMATION

We hope you have enjoyed reading this book – and that you will continue to in the coming years.

If you're a young writer who enjoys reading and creative writing, or the parent of an enthusiastic poet or story writer, do visit our website **www.youngwriters.co.uk**. Here you will find free competitions, workshops and games, as well as recommended reads, a poetry glossary and our blog.

If you would like to order further copies of this book, or any of our other titles, then please give us a call or visit **www.youngwriters.co.uk**.

Young Writers
Remus House
Coltsfoot Drive
Peterborough
PE2 9BF
(01733) 890066
info@youngwriters.co.uk

 @YoungWritersUK    @YoungWritersCW